To: _______________________

From: _______________________

We Belong To Allah

Copyright © 2025 Emma L. Halim
Illustrations by Herry Prihamdani
Sung by Oualid El Makami

ISBN: 978-0-6454064-9-8 (Paperback)
ISBN: 978-0-6457959-0-5 (Hardcover)
ISBN: 978-0-6457959-1-2 (E-book)

This book is a work of fiction. Names, characters, places, and incidents are either the product of the author's imagination or are used fictitiously and any resemblance to actual people, events or locales is entirely coincidental.

Editor: Khadijah Hayley
First printing edition 2025
Published by
Emma L. Halim

We Belong To Allah

Written by
Emma L. Halim

Sung by
Oualid El Makami

Illustrated by
Herry Prihamdani

Dedication

To all the animal lovers out there!

Just like Allah ﷻ created us all unique and special, every animal has its own quirks and charms, too!

Whether it's a chatty frog or a singing bird, it's up to us to show them love and kindness.

The Companions around the Prophet ﷺ asked:
"O Allah's Messenger ﷺ! Is there a reward for us in serving the animals?"
He ﷺ replied: "Yes, there is a reward for serving any living creature."

(Hadith: Sahih Muslim)

Come sing with Buraidah and his friends!

Scan the QR code to listen to the song!

OR

Visit EMMALHALIM.com

I saw a little frog,
I wondered what's his name.

He seemed so happy sitting there,
As if it were a game.

I'd like to take him home,
Sit him in my room,

I wondered if at night,
Would he 'ribbit' at the moon?

"I belong to Allah,"
I thought I heard him say.

His ribbit was so loud and strong
—I couldn't turn away.

I thought, you know, he's right,

As much as I liked him so,

He belongs to Allah

—and to our Lord, Allah, alone.

We belong to Allah,
We belong to Allah.
No matter where we are,
He takes good care of us.

We belong to Allah,
We belong to Allah.

No matter where we are,
We all belong to Allah.

I saw a little bird,
It seemed to smile at me.

I wondered if she'd like to come,
And share a cup of tea.

She'd fly into my room,
I'd name her **Breezy Bree.**
We'd chirp and chat all day
—as we sip our cups of tea.

"Why thank you very much.
That's so kind of you, I **know.**
But I belong to Allah
—and in the trees I like to **roam.**"

I thought, you know, she's right,
As much as I liked her **so,**
She belongs to Allah
—and to our Lord, Allah, **alone.**

We belong to Allah,
We belong to Allah.
No matter where we are
—He takes good care of us.

We belong to Allah,
We belong to Allah.
No matter where we are
—we all belong to Allah.

I saw a little ant,
He crawled upon my shoe.

Perhaps this was a sign,
He'd like to live in my room.

We'd be good friends, I think,
I'd name him Matey Mate.

We'd chat and chill all day
—while eating sweets and cake.

"Thank you for the invite,"
Matey Mate called out to me,

"but I belong to Allah
—He's the only One for me."

I thought, you know, he's right,
As much as I liked him so,
He belongs to Allah
—and to our Lord, Allah, alone.

We belong to Allah,
We belong to Allah.
No matter where we are,
—He takes good care of us.

We belong to **Allah**,
We belong to **Allah**.
No matter where we are
—we all belong to **Allah**.

Continue the Fun!

Can You Find...

 a pink balloon

 a blue and green bird

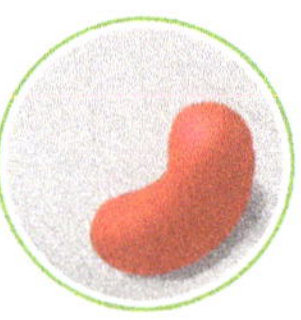 a red jellybean

 a red ladybird

 an orange fish

 a green teapot

Enjoy your free bonus printables!

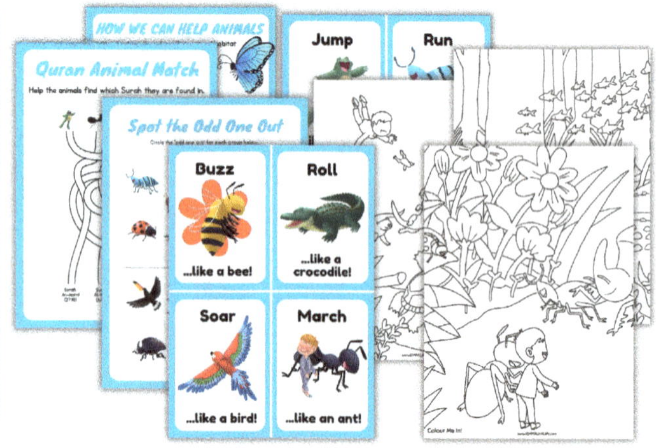

They go 'bee-autifully' with this book,
Alhamdulillah!

Meet the Illustrator

"Assalaamu 'alaykum!
I'm Herry, from Indonesia!

As a child, I loved drawing and reading story books.
Now I get to illustrate them, Alhamdulillah!"

Herry has fast become a much-loved and respected children's book illustrator, whose work can be found in books from various publishers worldwide. He has made a name for himself with his colourful characters and unique storytelling abilities, which range from both awe-inspiring to downright hilarious!

When he's not creating some new masterpiece, you can find him at City Park with his son and daughter.

And just in case you're wondering, his favourite animals are otters, cats, rabbits, guinea pigs, squirrels... ok, let's just say he loves ALL animals, shall we?!

Love Herry's illustrations in this book?
Let him know!
You can find him here:
@HERRY.EYI

Herry Prihamdani

Meet the Singer

"Assalaamu 'alaykum!
I'm Oualid, from Morocco!

I discovered I could sing when I was 7 years old, and now I get to sing every day, Alhamdulillah!"

Oualid is an internationally-recognised singer, songwriter, and producer, who spends his days creating songs with messages of hope and peace.

He encourages children to:
"Chase your dreams, whatever they are, don't forget to pray, and always remember Allah during your day."

When he's not whipping up some new tune, you can find him at the beach, enjoying the sunset with his wife and little baby.

When asked about his favourite animal, Oualid said:
"The fox!"

Want to hear more of Oualid's amazing songs? Check out his YouTube Channel:

OUALID EL MAKAMI

Oualid El Makami

Meet the Author

"Assalaamu 'alaykum!
I'm EMMA, from Australia!

When I was a kid, I loved coming up with fun stories and singing songs. Now I get to write them all down and share them with you, Alhamdulillah!"

Growing up on a farm in a tiny town in Australia, Emma has always loved animals. After school, she would often go for long walks along the creek, singing her heart out to any sheep, bird, dog, or cat who was kind (or rather, brave!) enough to listen.

As an adult, that love continues and she strives to teach kiddoes the importance of being kind to Allah's creatures—just like the Prophet Muhammad (peace be upon him) has taught us.

As an award-winning author, songwriter, and educator, Emma likes to put a fresh twist on faith-based resources. Whether at home or in the classroom, her books, songs, and educational resources are known for their quirky storytelling, memorable illustrations, and messages of friendship and good character. Best of all, they're simple for parents and teachers – and FUN for kids!

Want to hear more about Emma's songs and books?
Find her here:
@EMMALHALIM

Emma L. Halim

To My Family

First and foremost, I thank Allah ﷻ for allowing me to perform what I pray is a good deed. Ameen. I am so grateful to Him for all His blessings upon me and my family, Alhamdulillah.

Big hugs and thank you's to my kiddoes—my 'luvs' H and H—for encouraging me to keep writing day after day. Also, to my hubby, who's always supporting my kooky ideas and helping around the house so I have time to pursue my projects! May Allah ﷻ reward you all with Jannah Firdaus. Ameen.

Many thanks are also due to my mum and dad, and grandparents, who all gave me such a wonderful childhood, which I often ponder over as I write!

-Emma

More AWESOME Books and Songs by Emma!

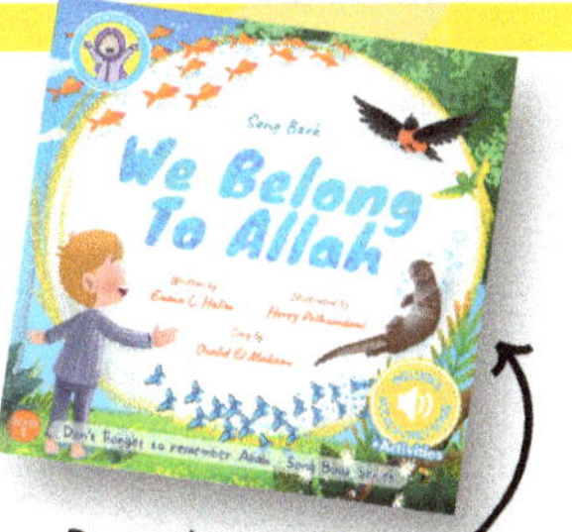

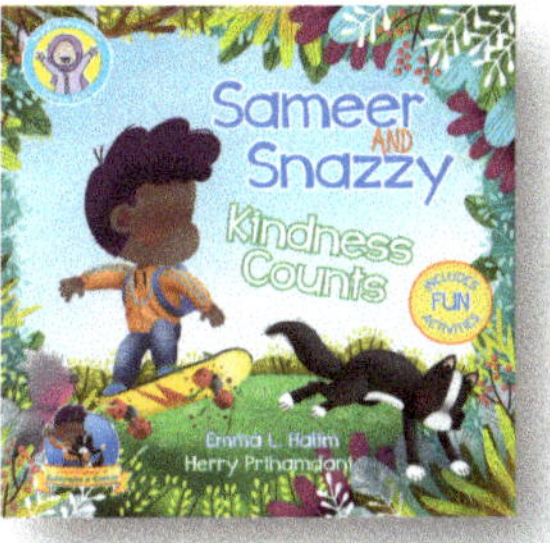

Learn about empathy and helping others!

Learn about Hajj!

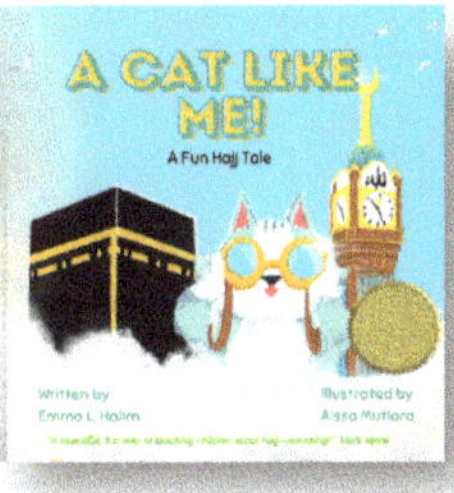

Ponder over Allah's Greatness!

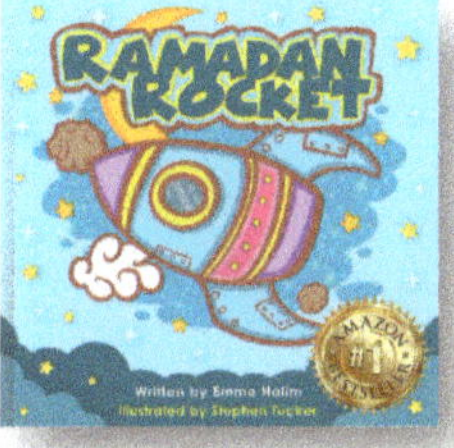

Use dhikr to help overcome anxiety!

Sing along while encouraging a growth mindset!

Introduce the sunnah of moon sighting!

Vocals-only songs for kids and parents alike!
Perfect for at home or in school.